THE GREAT DETECTIVE
SHERLOCK HOLMES
— THE MOST FORMIDABLE LADY NEMESIS —

THE GREAT DETECTIVE
SHERLOCK HOLMES
— THE MOST FORMIDABLE LADY NEMESIS —

The Chivalrous Thief from France

Moon hanging high in the evening sky, a masked thief dressed in all black was climbing quietly along the pipes on the exterior wall of a building, moving towards the third floor.

At the same time, two heads **poked out** from behind a dark street corner across the building, watching every move of the thief in black. These two heads belonged to none other than the famous Scotland Yard detective duo, Gordon "Gorilla" Riller and Carlson Fox.

As soon as the thief in black disappeared through a window on the third floor, Gorilla flashed his torch a few times to signal the police officers hiding a few blocks down the road. Gorilla and Fox then ran *discreetly* towards the building. Standing by behind the building, the two men waited anxiously for the thief in black to step into their trap.

poke(d) out (動+介) 探出、伸出   discreetly (副) 小心翼翼地、暗中地

A moment later, the thief's head poked out from the window, taking a cautious look downwards before hopping onto the exterior wall again to **descend** along the pipes.

"Catch him!" yelled Gorilla as the police siren began blaring through the quiet streets.

The police officers that were hiding three blocks down the road rushed at once towards the building where the thief in black was climbing down.

Although taken by surprise, the thief in black quickly **regained composure** then pulled out a whip and flicked it upwards, catching onto the pipes of the neighbouring building. With an agile leap, the thief in black swung cross the street towards the neighbouring building like a monkey jumping from one tree to another.

hop(ping) (動) 跳　descend (動) 往下　siren (名) 警號　blaring (blare) (動) 鳴響
regain(ed) composure (動+名) 恢復鎮靜　whip (名) 長皮鞭　flick(ed) (動) 輕輕揮動
4　agile (形) 敏捷的、靈活的

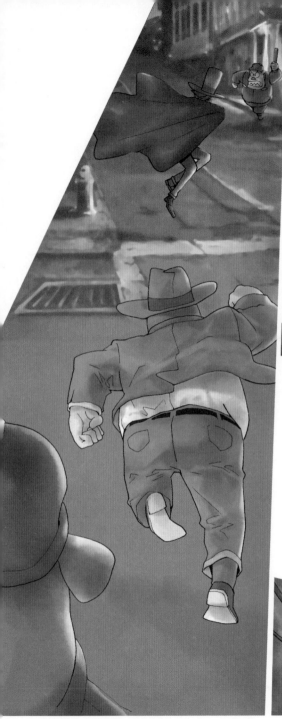

"Go after him! Don't let him get away!" shouted Gorilla.

After a steady landing, the thief in black flicked the whip upwards once again, this time catching the **railings** on the roof.

railing(s) (名) 欄杆

Several swift steps up the exterior wall and the thief in black had already climbed onto the roof. With a few more flicks of the whip, the thief in black leapt left and right then vanished into the night.

The next evening, Watson pushed open the front door and ran excitedly into the living room, "Holmes, have you heard the news? According to the newspaper,

vanish(ed) into (動+副) 消失得無影無蹤

the **infamous** masked thief, **Arsène Lupin**, has come to London and he is **burgling** around the city."

"Yes, I've heard," replied Holmes sleepily while *lounging* on the sofa.

"He has carried out so many robberies in the past half year that even Gorilla and Fox are *at a loss*!" exclaimed Watson, raising his voice a pitch higher.

"Yes, I've heard." With his eyes half shut, Holmes looked as though he was about to fall asleep.

"He is, apparently, known to be a **chivalrous** thief in France. Just like **Robin Hood**, he steals from the rich and gives to the poor. The French police are so *hard on his heels* that he has come to London to get away from them."

infamous (形) 臭名昭著的　Arsène Lupin (人名) 亞森羅蘋　burgling (burgle) (動) 入室盜竊
lounging (lounge) (動) 懶洋洋地躺着　at a loss (片語) 束手無策
chivalrous (形) 行俠仗義的　Robin Hood (人名) 羅賓漢　hard on his heels (習) 窮追

"Yes, I've heard," said Holmes as he let out a huge yawn.

Something did not feel right to Watson. Usually, Holmes would immediately jump off the sofa in excitement and discuss enthusiastically with Watson when such a topic headlined the newspapers. So why was Holmes so completely uninterested in this masked thief?

"I know him." Holmes's nonchalant utterance broke off Watson's train of thought.

"What?" screamed the

I know him.

enthusiastically (副) 熱切地、狂熱地　nonchalant (形) 漠不關心地、冷淡的
utterance (名) 說話

surprised Watson.

"I was **commissioned** by a wealthy French businessman and went up against Lupin three years ago."

"Oh? How come you've never mentioned him before?"

"He's an **opponent** that I'd prefer not to meet again.

If he weren't burgling around London, I would've wanted to wash him off my memory..." said Holmes as he swallowed back the words on the tip of his tongue.

"I see." Although curious, Watson could tell from his old partner's reaction that Holmes's encounter with Lupin must have been an unpleasant one. If Holmes did not wish to talk about it, then there must be a good reason and Watson *knew better than to* **pry**. However, both Watson and Holmes were unaware at this moment that the shadow of Lupin was *lurking* nearby and a storm was about to be **unleashed**.

"Instead of talking about this masked thief from France, why don't you take a look at this letter instead? A masked man is also mentioned in the letter," said Holmes as he took out a piece of paper from his pocket and handed it to Watson.

"Another masked man?" wondered Watson aloud as he took the letter from Holmes.

A short note was written on the piece of paper. It had no date, no signature and no address.

Dear Mr. Holmes,

Greetings!

Because of an important matter that must be discussed with you, a gentleman will be visiting your house at 7:45 tonight. We have heard how you helped resolve a *tricky* situation recently for a member of a royal family in Europe. This account of you we have from reliable sources received. We know you are one to be trusted upon.

Due to certain reasons, the visitor will be wearing a mask. We mean no *disrespect*.

tricky (形) 棘手的、難辦的　　disrespect (名) 不尊敬、對……無禮

11

"What a strange note," said Watson after he finished reading. "The note said the visitor is going to come here wearing a mask. Who do you suppose has sent this note?"

"Someone handed this note to the landlady this afternoon, asking her to pass it to me," said Holmes.

"Just a piece of paper? Was there an envelope?"

"No."

"No envelope? This messenger is very cautious indeed," analysed Watson.

"Yes, because including an extra item would be the same as leaving an extra clue for us to investigate upon. Merely *jotting down* the **gist** of the matter on a piece of paper is certainly the simplest and most straightforward."

"What can you tell from this piece of paper then?" asked Watson, expecting that his old partner must have thoroughly inspected the piece of paper already.

"I want to hear your thoughts first," said Holmes with a **shrewd** smile. Apparently, he wanted to

jot(ting) down (片語動) 寫下　　gist (名) 重點　　shrewd (形) 精明的、狡猾的

challenge Watson to a game of deduction .

"You wish to test me again?" said Watson as he cast a sidelong glance at Holmes before picking up the piece of paper for a closer look. "Hmmm… This is a beautiful piece of paper. The texture is very strong and **stiff**. It's probably not cheap at all."

"You have a sharp eye," praised Holmes.

"The person who uses this paper must be rather well off," said Watson.

"Very accurate analysis," said Holmes with a smile. "Why don't you hold it in front of the lamp and take a look?"

"Is there a watermark on the paper?" asked Watson as he held the paper near the lamp, only

deduction (名) 推理　stiff (形) 挺的、硬的　well off (形) 富有的
watermark (名) 水印

13

to find the alphabets "Eg.P.Gt." at the lower right corner. "Okay, I see a watermark. Could they be the initials of the writer?"

"No," replied Holmes. "'Gt.' is short for the German word 'Gessellschaft', just like 'Co.' is short for 'Company' in English. 'P.' stands for the German word 'Papier', which means 'paper' in English. As for 'Eg.', I've looked it up and it is short for 'Egria', which is a German-speaking country in Bohemia. And it so happens that Egria is famous for producing glass and high quality paper."

"If that's the case, this piece of paper must have been produced in Bohemia," said Watson.

"Yes. I also know that this note was written by a German."

"How did you figure that out?" asked Watson.

Holmes took the note and pointed at a line, "'This

alphabet(s) (名) 英文字母　Bohemia (地名) 波希米亞

account of you we have from reliable sources received.'
Don't you find this sentence rather peculiar?"

Watson thought for a moment and finally understood,
"The word order is very strange. It should be more
like, 'We have received this account of you from
reliable sources.'"

"Precisely. A Frenchman or a Russian would not
have written such a sentence. Only a German would
write in this word order," analysed Holmes. "Since
it is very hard to buy high quality Bohemian paper
in England, I've deduced from the peculiarly written
sentence and the paper's country of origin that the
writer must be a wealthy German."

Just at that moment, sharp noises of clip-clopping
hooves sounded from outside the window.

Holmes walked towards the window then said with
a chuckle, "It appears that our honourable masked
guest has arrived. Come take a look, Watson. The two
horses pulling the carriage are of high quality and the
carriage itself is a top-of-the-class, four-wheel model.

peculiar (形) 古怪的   clip-clop(ping) hooves (習) 噠噠的馬蹄聲

Even if this case turns out to be most **frivolous**, we should still be able to reap in a good amount of earnings."

frivolous (形) 無謂的、無意義的　reap (動) 獲得、收穫

The Mysterious Masked Man

A moment later, deep, weighty footsteps could be heard from the corridor outside. As soon as they had taken a halt, a few ***authoritative*** knocks sounded at the door.

Watson might not be as skilled as Holmes in identifying people from the noises they make, but even Watson could tell from those pretentious-sounding footsteps and knocks that their guest tonight must be a **burly** man who was in the habit of putting on airs.

"Come in!" shouted Holmes.

Pushing open the front door was a large-built gentleman towering at six feet six inches in height. Even though he was wearing a heavy coat and a **massive** shawl that reached all the way down to his knees, the broadness of his chest was still apparent underneath the thick layers of clothing. The

---

halt (名) 停止　　authoritative (形) 權威性的　　pretentious (形) 造作的、自命不凡的
burly (形) 魁梧的、強壯的、結實的　　put(ting) on airs (片語動) 擺架子
massive (形) 巨大的　　shawl (名) 披肩

mysterious mask covering his face made him look all the more **imposing** too. Anyone who walked past a man like this on the streets at night would surely be **intimidated** by his appearance. However, the **vulgar emerald breastpin** on his shawl and his *calf-high* boots had **given him away**, suggesting that he was perhaps more *flamboyant* than dangerous.

Taking a look first at Holmes then at Watson, the burly masked man appeared to be uncertain to whom he should speak. He settled on Holmes at the end and said with a very heavy German accent, "Have you received my note? I have notified you about my visit."

Holmes nodded and said, "How may I address you?"

The burly masked man turned to Watson. Although his exact expression was obscured by the mask, the doubt in his eyes was clearly visible.

"I would like to speak with you alone," said the burly masked man to Holmes.

"This is Dr. Watson. He is a good friend and a reliable partner in my work. If he is not allowed to

imposing (形) 威嚴的、敬畏的　　intimidate(d) (動) 嚇倒、望而生畏
vulgar (形) 庸俗的　emerald (名) 綠寶石　breastpin (名) 襟針　calf-high (形) 高及小腿
give(n) him away (片語動) 泄露了、出賣了　flamboyant (形) 虛張聲勢的、浮誇

take part, then you leave me no choice but to decline the **commission**." Holmes then pointed to a chair and said, "Please take a seat."

Holmes's tone was calm yet firm and **dignified** at the same time. Knowing that an appeal would be **futile**, the burly masked man shot a **frosty** glance at Watson before sitting down on the chair.

"I am from Bohemia. You may address me as **Count** Von Kramm," the burly masked man introduced himself.

A wealthy man from Bohemia, which is what Holmes has deduced from the note! Holmes is right on the dot once again, thought Watson.

"How may I be of help to you, Count Von Kramm?" asked Holmes, neither too eager nor too cold.

commission (名) 委託   dignified (形) 威嚴的   futile (形) 無用的、白費心機
frosty (形) 冷冷的   Count (名) 伯爵   on the dot (片) 全中、完全正確

The count shifted his sitting posture a little before *assuming* a serious tone, "**Discretion**! I demand your utter discretion because this matter may greatly influence the future development of European history. May I trust you two gentlemen to keep this a secret for two years?"

Holmes **shrugged** his shoulders and said, "Of course. But two years of secrecy is too short for a matter of such importance. How about we promise to keep this a secret *eternally*?"

Watson nodded in agreement, "Eternal sounds fine to me."

It was not unusual for clients to exaggerate the importance of their own cases. Holmes and Watson could tell from years of experience that a matter which "may greatly influence the future development of European history" would most likely turn out to be something far less significant.

Reassured by their promises to eternal secrecy, the count pushed his mask up lightly with his index finger

assuming (assume) (動) 換用、裝出　discretion (名) 守口如瓶
shrug(ged) (動) 聳一聳　eternally (副) 永久地　reassure(d) (動) 消除疑慮、使安心　21

and said, "Please forgive me for not taking off my mask. The prestigious status of my employer must not be known. He does not wish for you to figure out his identity from my presence. But I can tell you this truth, that Count Von Kramm is just a **pseudonym** for the use of this case."

"It is fine. I am aware of that already." Holmes shrugged his shoulders again, indicating that he was not bothered by such arrangements.

"This is a very delicate situation and we must be meticulous with every detail. Any mistake would create a scandal that would shock the world and *disgrace* the crown of a certain European country," said the count with his voice pressed low.

Watson glanced over to Holmes, only to find Holmes listening to the count with an expressionless face. In fact, Holmes's eyes were half shut, looking as though

prestigious (形) 尊貴的、聲名顯赫的　pseudonym (名) 假名
meticulous (形) 嚴密的、一絲不苟　disgrace (動) 使蒙受恥辱

he was about to fall asleep. Since Holmes gave no response, the masked count cut straight to the point, "To be more precise, this matter concerns the House of **Ormstein**, which is the line of the **hereditary** kings of Bohemia!"

Watson noticed that Holmes's eyeballs twitched a bit under his half-shut eyelids upon hearing those words. Perhaps the masked count had finally brought up something of interest to Holmes. Holmes cast a sidelong glance at the count with his sleepy eyes and

Ormstein (名稱) 奧姆斯坦
hereditary (形) 世襲的

said, "I understand that it must not be easy for a king to *demean* himself so *humbly*, but should Your Majesty refuse to tell me the whole truth, the advice that I can offer will be limited."

demean (動) 貶低身份、紆尊降貴　　humbly (副) 謙遜地、卑躬屈膝地

The masked count was so **taken aback** by Holmes's words that he quickly stood up from the chair and stared down at Holmes, who was sitting lazily on the sofa. His face **flushed** red, the count wanted to shout at Holmes but he was at a loss. Meanwhile, Holmes closed his eyes and took a puff on his pipe, completely ignoring his honourable guest. After a tense moment of silent standstill, the masked count **gave in** and began pacing back and forth in the living room. All of a sudden, he stopped pacing and tore the mask off his face, tossing it onto the floor before announcing dramatically, "I am the king. I shall no longer hide my identity. Why should I anyway? It's pointless to try to hide my identity in front of the famous great detective."

take(n) aback (片語動) 嚇一跳、出乎意料　　flushed (形) 發紅的
gave (give) in (片語動) 投降、讓步、放棄

"That's right, Grand Duke of Cassel-Felstein," said Holmes slowly, enunciating clearly every syllable of the visitor's real name.

The true identity of the burly masked man turned out to be the Grand Duke of Cassel-Felstein, the hereditary king of Bohemia!

Holmes is amazing indeed! All he had to do was **put on a front** *and he was able to figure out the real identity of the masked count in no time,* thought Watson. Holmes only pretended to be uninterested in the matter at hand in order to

Grand Duke (名) 大公爵　　enunciating (enunciate) (動) 發音　　syllable (名) 音節
put on a front (習) 裝模作樣

provoke the masked count to reveal more information. Holmes was especially savvy with this kind of mind games. A person in need of help would naturally try to attract the attention of the one from whom he wished to **solicit** help. A child in need of his mother's attention might cry as loudly as he could. A boy wishing to attract the attention of his dream girl might make it a point to be within her line of sight at all times. A pet craving for attention from its owner might leave its droppings in noticeable places. Here was a king who was used to endless **showers of** admiration and attention. But when this king was in need of Holmes's attention, Holmes responded with indifference, which *irritated* the king so much that it drove him to reveal his royal identity at the end.

provoke (動) 激起、挑釁　savvy (形) 精於　solicit (動) 請求、徵求
droppings (名) 糞便　shower(s) of (名) 大量的　irritate(d) (動) 刺激、激怒

The Alluring Singer Irene Adler

After regaining his composure, the King of Bohemia sat down again and lightly wiped his forehead with his hand, "I hope you will understand. I have never dealt with a private investigator before, so I really have no clue how to handle this kind of situation. But since this matter is so sensitive that it could affect the course of my future, I must see to it myself."

"Is that why **Your Majesty** have come here in **disguise**?" asked Holmes.

"Yes."

"But Your Majesty's carriage and clothing are far too conspicuous. Perhaps you may want to consider a more subdued presentation," remarked Holmes with a hint of sarcasm.

---

composure (名) 鎮定、冷靜　Your Majesty (名稱) 陛下　disguise (名) 偽裝、喬裝打扮
conspicuous (形) 引人注意的、顯眼的　subdued (形) 低調的　sarcasm (名) 諷刺、挖苦

"As I have said already, I'm not used to this kind of situation. But I can assure you that only a few of my trusty **attendants** know about this secret trip of mine from Prague to London."

"May I ask what brings Your Majesty to my humble home?"

"It's a long story. **The short of it** is, I met a beautiful woman named Irene Adler when I visited France five years ago, but it was only later that I realised she was but a **gold digger**."

"That name sounds familiar. Let me look it up," said Holmes as he stood up then walked to the file cabinet to pull out a thick folder and started thumbing

attendant(s) (名) 隨從　　Prague (地名) 布拉格
the short of it (片) 簡單地說、長話短說、總而言之　　gold digger (名) 貪錢的女人

through it. Watson recognised the folder right away. It was Holmes's index of **personalities**, a compilation of biographies on interesting people of all sorts that Holmes had collected throughout the years.

"Here it is," said Holmes as he stopped at a page. "Irene Adler, born in 1868 in the state of New Jersey in America, a renowned alto… Oh wow, this is amazing! She was a principal singer at the Royal Opera in France but left the company half a year ago. She is now living in London."

Music had always been a keen passion of Holmes's. In fact, he was so fond of music that he even attended a violin concert in the middle of an investigation one time*. Watson could instantly sense the enthusiasm in Holmes now that they knew the king's case concerned a famous singer.

Sure enough, before the king even had a chance to say anything, Holmes was already asking eagerly, "Your Majesty, were you courting her and wrote her some love letters that you would like me to retrieve?"

*For details, please refer to *The Great Detective Sherlock Holmes ⑨ The Great Robbery*

personalities (personality) (名) 人物　　compilation (名) 編輯、匯編
biographies (biography) (名) 傳記、個人經歷　　renowned (形) 知名的
alto (名) 女低音　　principal (形) 首席　　retrieve (動) 取回

"How amazing! You've almost guessed it right."

"Did you marry her in secret?"

"No."

"Is she holding onto some legal documents that are unfavourable to you?"

"No."

"Then I don't understand. What proof does she have that those letters are real if she were to threaten or blackmail you with them?"

"It's my handwriting."

"But that could be **imitated**."

"I used my private stationery."

"She could've stolen them."

imitate(d) (動) 模仿

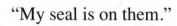
"My seal is on them."

"That could be forged."

"She has my photo."

"She could've bought it."

"It's not a portrait of me."

"I beg your pardon?"

"It's a photo of me and her together."

"What?" exclaimed the surprised Holmes. "Your Majesty had been too careless."

"I was blinded by love at that time. I was so head over heels in love with her that I lost my sense of judgment," said the king as he covered his face with his hand regretfully.

"I'm sorry to say this, Your Majesty, but you dived into this dangerous trap yourself."

---

forge(d) (動) 偽造　　head over heels in love (習) 墜入愛河

"You don't have to remind me. I was but Crown Prince back then. I was far too young. Even now I am only thirty years old."

"The photo must be retrieved then," said Holmes.

"I've tried but failed."

"Just buy it back. It's worth spending the money."

"I wouldn't be so distressed if she is willing to sell the photo."

"Then steal it."

"I've tried stealing it five times already. Twice I've hired someone to break into her home but could not find it anywhere despite searching every corner of the house. Once we switched her luggage while she was travelling but couldn't find it in her bags. We've even tried **snatching** her purse on the street twice but still had no luck finding the photo," said the **dejected** king.

snatch(ing) (動) 搶走、奪走　dejected (形) 垂頭喪氣、沮喪

33

"Do you have any leads or clues on the photo?"

"None whatsoever."

At this point, Holmes could not help but chortle, "This woman is amazing! What *a barrel of laughs*!"

"This is no laughing matter. That photo can ruin me," grumbled the king.

"I apologise," said Holmes, barely wiping the grin off his face. "If she is not after your money, what good is the photo to her?"

"She wants to destroy me."

"Destroy you? How?"

"I am getting married soon."

"So I've read in the newspapers."

"My fiancée is the second daughter of the King of Scandinavia.

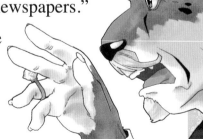

---

chortle (動) 哈哈大笑　　a barrel of laughs (片) 有趣、搞笑　　grumble(d) (動) 抱怨
grin (名) 咧嘴笑　　Scandinavia (地名) 斯堪的納維亞

Her family is very strict and she is a sensitive, delicate soul who cannot handle any unpleasant surprises. She would definitely call off the wedding if she were to find out that I once courted a songstress," said the king.

"Has Miss Adler taken any action?"

"She is threatening to send the photo to my fiancée," said the troubled king. "Irene Adler is a woman of her word, so I know she would absolutely do it. Mr. Holmes, you must understand that though her heart may be *tender*, her determination is rock-solid. She is also very **headstrong**. She will **go to great lengths** to stop me from marrying another woman. That's Irene Adler for you!"

"A very fascinating woman indeed," admired Holmes but quickly realised his **faux pas** as soon as those words slipped out of his mouth. Putting on a serious face, Holmes asked, "Has she sent the photo yet?"

---

call off (片語動) 取消、解除　court(ed) (動) 追求、交往　songstress (名) 歌女
tender (形) 溫柔的　rock-solid (形) 如石般堅硬、堅強　headstrong (形) 固執的
go to great lengths (習) 不顧一切地　faux pas (名) 失言、失禮

"Not yet."

"How do you know?"

"She told me she plans to send it on the day the wedding is announced officially, which is next Monday."

"So we still have three days," said Holmes with great enthusiasm. "That should be enough time to track down the photo."

Looks like my old partner is completely captivated by this woman whom he has yet to meet, thought Watson.

"Your Majesty, will you be staying in London in the meantime?" asked Holmes.

"Of course. I must retrieve that photo before I leave," replied the king. "I've used the name Count Von Kramm for my booking at the Langham Hotel. You can find me there once you've come upon any information."

"Very well," said Holmes as he lightly rubbed his nose. "Your Majesty, I'm sure you are aware that my fees are rather high."

"How high exactly?" asked the king.

"Pretty high. And an advance deposit is required."

captivate(d) (動) 迷倒、吸引　　advance deposite (形+名) 訂金

Watson let out a **smirk** in secret after hearing those words. Holmes's attitude towards money had always been very nonchalant, often helping the poor for free. However, if the clients happened to be rich and powerful, not only would Holmes ask for a deposit, he would not hesitate to **drain** their wallets by demanding an additional **hefty** payment upon completing the investigation.

"Deposit?" said the king as he took out two heavy leather bags from under his coat and placed them **gingerly** on the table. "I have with me 300 pounds in gold coins and 700 pounds in banknotes . Will this be enough?" asked the king.

smirk (名) 詭秘的笑、暗笑　　drain (動) 耗盡　　hefty (形) 大的、可觀的
gingerly (副) 小心翼翼地、謹慎地

37

Watson could not help but widen his eyes because the amount offered by the king had far exceeded his expectation. Holmes, on the contrary, squinted his eyes. After taking a good look at the king, Holmes casually scribbled something in his notebook then tore the page and handed it to the king, "This amount is not enough as a deposit, actually, but I shall make it an exception, seeing that you are the King of Bohemia. Your Majesty, here is your receipt."

Watson nearly **keeled over** in surprise upon hearing Holmes's words. He could not believe that Holmes had the audacity to utter such a bald-faced exaggeration! The amount on the table was almost the same as their total income from the past two years.

squint(ed) (動) 瞇着眼　scribble(d) (動) 草草地寫　keel(ed) over (片語動) 突然倒下
audacity (名) 大膽、放肆　bald-faced (形) 厚顏無恥　exaggeration (名) 誇大

"Can you tell me where does Miss Adler live?" asked Holmes casually.

Relieved that Holmes had accepted his deposit, the king replied, "She lives in a place called Briony Lodge on Serpentine Avenue in St. John's Wood."

Holmes quickly jotted down the address then asked, "How big is the photo in question? Is it around six inches?"

"Yes, it is."

"Your Majesty, this is all the information I need," said Holmes as he picked up the mask on the floor and handed it back to the king. "Rest assured that you will be hearing good news from me very soon."

Although a sense of doubt still remained on his face,

lodge (名) 小居

the king gave Holmes a polite nod before taking his leave.

Soon after the weighty footsteps reached the bottom of the staircase, the clip-clopping of hooves sounded from below as the carriage horses **trotted** away from Baker Street. Once the noises had trailed off, Watson turned to Holmes, "The king was so **generous** with the deposit, yet you still acted like the amount was too little. You're unbelievable!"

"Generous? To a king, this amount isn't even enough to buy a painting to hang on the wall in his toilet," said Holmes without moving a muscle on his face.

"But to you, this is a massive amount of money," argued Watson.

Instead of responding to Watson's remark, Holmes suddenly leaned close to Watson's face and asked, "Have you eaten dinner

trot(ted) (動) 馬兒慢跑　　trail(ed) off (片語動) 逐漸消失　　generous (形) 大方、慷慨

40

yet?"

The **baffled** Watson replied, "Not yet."

"Ahahahaha! I'm rich! I'm **filthy rich**!" exploded Holmes into a roaring laughter. "Let's celebrate with an **extravagant** feast at the most expensive French restaurant in town!" No longer needed to hold his laughter in his stomach, Holmes unleashed his **boisterous elation**, which was now **throbbing** in Watson's ear.

It was only then that Watson realised Holmes only pretended to be nonchalant when he was talking about the fees with the king. Holmes might have appeared to be *aloof* on the outside, but he was actually jumping in excitement on the inside, because this deposit alone was plenty enough to cover all of their regular expenses for two years.

---

baffled (形) 困惑的　filthy rich (習) 發大財、極之富有　extravagant (形) 奢侈的、昂貴的
boisterous (形) 喧鬧的　elation (名) 狂歡、興高采烈　throb(bing) (動) 震響、振動
aloof (形) 莫不關心的

"So how do you plan to approach this case?" asked Watson when Holmes's laughter finally dwindled to a chuckle.

"Finding where a woman has hidden a photo shouldn't be too hard. I'll go over there tomorrow and see what I can gather on this Irene Adler first before coming up with a more specific plan." Still enjoying his profitable moment, Holmes had no idea that he was about to meet the most formidable woman that he would ever face in his life. Holmes's encounter with her would not only bring Holmes to gain new respect for women in general but also trick Holmes into a trap that was devised by his long-time nemesis, Dr. M!

dwindle(d) (動) 減退　　formidable (形) 極難對付的、可怕的
nemesis (名) 剋星、死對頭、勁敵

The Extraordinary Encounter at the Church

It was already three o'clock in the afternoon the next day when Watson returned to Baker Street from a home visit. Watson was very much **intrigued** last night when the King of Bohemia brought over his case. As fascinating as any royalty scandal might be, Watson was actually more curious about the singer named Irene Adler, secretly hoping that he could meet her in person soon.

It's past three o'clock already. How come Holmes is not home yet? thought Watson after taking out his pocket watch for a look. Before Watson left home this morning, Holmes had specifically asked Watson to meet back at the flat at this time.

When it was almost four o'clock, the front door suddenly opened and in came a bearded drunkard who appeared to be a carriage driver dressed in tattered clothes. Although Watson was pretty familiar with

intrigue(d) (動) 使好奇　　drunkard (名) 酒鬼、醉漢
tattered (形) 破爛的

Holmes's disguise expertise by now, Watson still needed to take a long, good look at this man before he was certain that standing before him was his old partner.

"Sorry to have kept you waiting," smiled Holmes as he walked to his bedroom. After a few minutes, he came out of his room looking like his normal self again while letting out a cheerful laughter.

expertise (名) 專長

"Well? What have you found?" asked Watson anxiously.

"You would not believe the **extraordinary** encounter I've just had this morning," said Holmes with a pretentious chuckle.

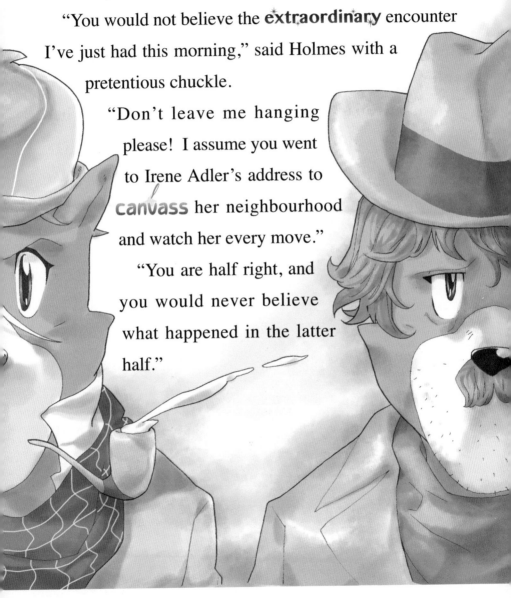

"Don't leave me hanging please! I assume you went to Irene Adler's address to **canvass** her neighbourhood and watch her every move."

"You are half right, and you would never believe what happened in the latter half."

extraordinary (形) 非凡的、令人驚奇的　canvass (動) 調查

"Do tell! Do tell!" urged Watson.

"This morning, I went to investigate around Serpentine Avenue while disguised as a carriage driver who was out of work. There I found a **mews** in an alley near Irene Adler's home. You see, ordinary working folks might be **crude** in their manners but they have a strong sense of camaraderie. The drivers there took sympathy in my unemployment and we started chatting."

"So what have you learnt?" asked Watson.

"I chatted with them while I helped them brushed their horses. They knew everything about the people living in the area like the back of their hands. They shared with me a good amount of gossips that

mews (名) 馬房、馬廄　crude (形) 粗魯的　camaraderie (名) 同僚間的互助精神、義氣

I did not care to know. After a while, I finally managed to **steer** the topic onto Irene Adler."

"What happened next?" Watson could not help but stretch his neck forward now that Holmes had finally reached the subject of interest.

"Those drivers could not stop admiring Irene Adler's beauty once we began talking about her. Apparently, she was also very generous with tipping so she was well liked by everyone. The drivers told me that she would ride a carriage everyday around five o'clock in the evening to sing at concerts then return home around seven o'clock for supper. She seldom leaves home besides that," said Holmes.

"That's not much of a discovery then," said the disappointed Watson.

"The best is yet to come, my dear Watson," said Holmes with a shrewd smile. "Those drivers also told

steer (動) 引導   stretch (動) 伸展

me that a man has been visiting her home very often lately."

"Oh?" A beautiful woman hooking up with a man? That sparked a curiosity in Watson right away.

"This man's name is Norton. He is tall and handsome, probably in his thirties. He is also a lawyer. A young and talented professional indeed," said Holmes.

"So she already has a young and talented professional as a boyfriend?" said the disappointed Watson as he recoiled his outstretched neck.

"What? Don't tell me that you're jealous?" Holmes could not help but tease Watson, "You always get so excited when you hear about an attractive woman, but this time is a bit too much, don't you think? You've never even set eyes on this Irene Adler."

"No, no, no!" Watson tried his best to reject Holmes's **accusation**, but his flushed cheeks just

hook(ing) up (片語動) 勾搭上　recoil(ed) (動) 縮起　tease (動) 嘲笑、戲弄
accusation (名) 指控、指責

gave him away.

With a wide grin on his face, Holmes stared amusingly at Watson, loving the look on Watson's face whenever Watson was embarrassed.

To draw Holmes's attention away from his flustered face, Watson immediately asked, "So what have you discovered about this man's background?"

"I didn't have time to investigate further, but the drivers were sure that this man is a lawyer because they have driven him to his law firm many times. After learning this, I have a feeling that this case might be more complicated than expected," said Holmes.

"How do you mean?"

"This is a worrying sign. Why is Irene Adler seeing this lawyer named Norton? If Norton is not her boyfriend, then that means Irene Adler is his client. I started thinking that she might've given the photo to him for safekeeping. It's certainly problematic if that's the case," said Holmes.

---

gave (give) him away (片語動) 出賣了、露出馬腳   flustered (形) 激動、着急、緊張
problematic (形) 困難的

"I see what you mean. A law firm is guarded with maximum security, not to mention the difficulty of finding a single photograph within the piles of documents."

"But it turned out that my worry was unnecessary."

"How come?"

"Because something completely unexpected happened afterwards." With a mysterious smile on his face, Holmes recounted his extraordinary encounter in detail.

After I left the mews, I went over to Briony Lodge for a look and found that it was a **splendid**, two-storey structure on a street corner

splendid (形) 很好、不俗

with a small garden in the back. There was a rather large window on the second floor, so large that one could see the people on the second floor if one were to look from across the street.

Just as I was **brooding** over why Irene Adler needed to see a lawyer, a two-seater carriage suddenly pulled up in front of Briony Lodge, then a gentleman quickly hopped off from the carriage.

brood(ing) (動) 苦思

This gentleman was a young, handsome man. He was most likely to be Norton. As though he was returning to his own home, he walked past the maid as soon as she had opened the door for him and went straight into the house by himself.

I pretended to be a **pedestrian**, walking back and forth and passing Briony Lodge three times. I could see Norton talking and waving his arms wildly on the second floor. He seemed to be very excited. I suspected that he was speaking to Irene Adler, but I could not see her at all.

He stepped out of the house half an hour later, but he appeared to be in a bigger hurry now than when he first arrived. He told the carriage driver who was waiting at the front door, "Drive as fast as you can, first to a law firm on Regent Street, then to St. Monica Church on Edgeware Road." His voice was so loud that I could

pedestrian (名) 行人

hear his every word clearly.

As I watched his carriage drive away, I began to wonder whether I should follow him. Just then, a small coach pulled up in front of Briony Lodge. Its door flew open before it even came to a complete stop. And almost at the same time, a woman in a demure dress shot out from the front door and hopped into the coach. The moment was so brief that I was not able to get a good look at the woman, but from her light and elegant movements, I could tell that she must be a charming creature that men would easily fall for.

To find out exactly where she was going, I quickly hid behind the coach to listen in.

"To St. Monica Church on Edgeware Road please. You shall earn half a gold coin if we could arrive within twenty minutes." Saying those words was a beautiful

---

demure (形) 端莊的　　shot (shoot) out (片語動) 衝出

voice, a voice so *melodic* that it could only belong to a singer. I was so captivated by this voice that was as sweet as wind chimes that the coach had already begun moving before I came back to my senses. It drove away in such high speed that I was genuinely **caught off guard**.

Fortunately, another carriage passed by just in time for me to **hail** it down. Before the driver had a chance to refuse his service to me since I was dressed in rags and tatters, I proposed my offer, "Drive to St. Monica Church on Edgeware Road. If you can make it there in twenty minutes, half a gold coin is yours."

While I was riding in the carriage, I could not help but wonder why Irene Adler and Norton needed to meet at the church if they had just seen each other at the house. As much as I tried, I just could not come up with any idea, but I was sure that there must be a reason behind. I knew that I simply could not miss this chance of finding the answer. And it really was my lucky day today, because my driver happened to be a *daredevil* who would do anything for money.

melodic (形) 悅耳的　caught (catch) off guard (片語) 措手不及　hail (動) 截(車)
rags and tatters (名) 破舊衣服、衣衫襤褸　daredevil (名) 不怕死的人

Speeding recklessly through the streets, we arrived at our destination in less than twenty minutes.

However, it turned out that London was full of daredevil drivers who would do anything for money. By the time of my arrival, both Norton's and Irene Adler's carriages were also parked in front of the church, their horses *panting* breathlessly and sweating *profusely*.

I began to worry that the church was only a **rendezvous point** and I would lose them if they were to go in from the front then leave from the back. This was a common tactic to **throw off** a **pursuer**. According to the king, this Irene Adler was so clever that she might have noticed my watching her already. Also, since the king had his men **sneaked up on** her several times before, her sense of awareness was probably more heightened than the average woman. I could not afford to lose track of them, so I quickly slipped into the church.

Besides Norton and Irene Adler, there was only a **vicar** in a white **robe** inside the poorly lit church. They

---

pant(ing) (動) 喘氣、喘息　　profusely (副) 大量地、不停地
rendezvous point (名) 見面地點、集合地點　　throw off (片語動) 擺脫　　pursuer (名) 追蹤者
sneak(ed) up on (片語動) 偷襲　　vicar (名) 牧師　　robe (名) 長袍、禮袍　　55

appeared to be in the middle of an argument, for they had not noticed my quiet entrance. To better hear their conversation, I pretended to be an *idler* who had just wandered into the church. I walked up quietly by the side <u>aisle</u>, making sure that both Irene Adler and Norton had their backs facing me so they could not see me. But

idler (名) 流浪漢、無業遊民　　aisle (名) 通道

the vicar noticed my presence right away and pointed his finger towards me, "There's a man over there."

Before I could figure out why the vicar needed to point me out, Irene Adler turned her head around slowly. It was then that I finally got a clear look at this woman who the king claimed to be as pretty as an angel. I have met all sorts of people in my life, many of which were gorgeous women, but none as exquisite and beguiling as Irene Adler. The king was right. I could definitely see from the look in her mesmerising eyes that she was a

exquisite (形) 美麗的、優雅的、精緻的　beguiling (形) 誘人
mesmerising (形) 令人着迷的

strong woman with a mind of her own. Those were the eyes of a clever and sophisticated woman, making her all the more unforgettably alluring. If it were not for those eyes, she would be nothing but just another ordinary pretty face.

I must have been *stunned* speechless for a few seconds. When I came back to my senses, Irene Adler had just finished saying something in Norton's ear then began walking towards me in a *graceful* manner. Had she seen through my disguise? I could not help but wonder. So I immediately pretended to be bored from wandering about, slowly turning my body around and hoping to make it out the door before my identity was exposed.

sophisticated (形) 懂得人情世故的、高雅的　　alluring (形) 迷人的、有魅力的
stunned (形) 驚呆、意想不到、震驚的　　graceful (形) 優雅的

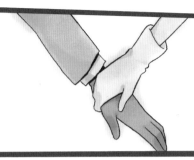

That was when the most shocking thing of all happened. A delicate hand suddenly took hold of my hand. I turned around only to find Irene Adler right before my eyes. As much as I tried to stay calm, I could imagine that my lips were probably quivering.

"Sir, can you please help me? It will take but three minutes of your time." Once again, I was caught off guard by Irene Adler's sweet sounding voice.

quiver(ing) (動) 顫抖

"What?" I did not understand what was going on.

"Please just lend me three minutes, otherwise it won't be legal," said Irene Adler with a smile.

Before I could even offer a reply, she had already dragged me before the vicar. Looking at me with her

dazzling eyes, she said to me, "Sir, you have a pair of honest eyes. They shall bring us good luck."

"Thank you for your help," said the young, handsome lawyer named Norton.

Before I could even figure out what they meant, I was already following

the vicar's words and making an **oath** *in a daze*. It turned out that those two **lovebirds** were in a hurry to get married but they did not have a witness, so my sudden appearance had saved their **ceremony**.

dazzling (形) 閃亮的、燦爛的　oath (名) 宣誓　in a daze (片語) 茫然、莫名其妙
lovebirds (名) 情侶　ceremony (名) 儀式

How **preposterous**! I actually became the wedding witness of my investigation target!

When the simple ceremony was complete, a **blissful** smile glowed on Irene Adler's *angelic* face. After thanking the vicar, she turned to me and leaned close to my face.

"Sir…" said the woman before she planted a light kiss on my cheek all of a sudden. "I am so happy to have you as our wedding witness. If it weren't for you, our wedding would have to be postponed." Upon saying those words, she *shoved* a gold coin into my hand as a token of thanks. Then the *newlyweds* happily hopped into their own carriages separately, leaving the stunned idler standing in the

preposterous (形) 荒謬的、愚蠢的　blissful (形) 喜悅的、幸福的　angelic (形) 天使般的
shove(d) (動) 塞到　newlyweds (名) 新婚夫婦

church by himself. Needless to say, that stunned idler was yours truly.

After narrating his encounter, Holmes could not help but continue to admire, "You know, Watson, that kiss that Irene Adler had pecked on my cheek made me realise that not only is she clever and beautiful, she also has a kind and gentle soul."

"Has that pretty face swept you off your feet so badly that you hit yourself on your head? How could you tell if someone's soul is kind or evil just by a kiss on the cheek?" said Watson as he cast a **dubious** sidelong glance at Holmes.

"No," disagreed Holmes *bluntly*. "But you must remember that I was an idler dressed in rags at that time, yet she bore no **resentment** towards having me,

---

peck(ed) (動) 輕吻   swept (sweep) you off your feet (片語) 使神魂顛倒
dubious (形) 懷疑的   bluntly (副) 直言地   resentment (名) 反感

a filthy man who smelled of horse manure, as her wedding witness and even planted a kiss on my cheek. Only a kind and gentle soul would do such a thing."

"Fair enough. So she has a kind and gentle soul. Let's not argue on that anymore," agreed Watson reluctantly.

"This kind and gentle soul also gave me a gold coin. To commemorate this extraordinary encounter, I shall hang it as a lucky charm on my pocket watch chain." Holmes let out a cheerful laughter as he flashed the radiant gold coin before Watson.

filthy (形) 骯髒的   reluctantly (副) 不情願地   commemorate (動) 紀念
radiant (形) 光芒四射的、金光閃閃的

Watson rolled his eyes and said, "Isn't it too early for you to be so happy? We still have no clue on the **whereabouts** of the photo."

"Patience, my dear Watson. Our next step is to look for the photo, and I need your help this time."

"Exactly what I was hoping for. I'd like to see for myself the striking beauty of this Irene Adler too."

"But it requires breaking the law."

"No problem."

"You might get caught."

"Don't mind if it's worth it."

"Should be worth it."

"At your beck and call."

---

clue (名) 線索　　whereabouts (名) 行蹤　　at your beck and call (習) 隨時候命

 "You are a good partner indeed."

 "So what do you need me to do?"

Holmes took off his hat, tossed it lightly towards the coat hanger and it landed securely on one of the hooks.

"You give it a try," said Holmes to Watson.

Watson's face was filled with questions, but he took

toss(ed) (動) 扔、抛

66

off his own hat and tossed it towards the coat hanger nevertheless. His hat **flipped** a few times in the air and also landed securely on one of the hooks.

"How amazing! Where did you learn how to do that?" asked Holmes astonishingly.

"It's nothing. I learnt how to throw hand **grenades** in the army," said Watson. "Now can you tell me how is tossing my hat related to stealing the photo?"

"Better not tell you now, or you might regret it later," replied Holmes with a cunning smile on his face.

Watson began to worry upon hearing Holmes's words. Exactly what kind of laws were they about to break? Although Watson trusted Holmes wholeheartedly, he still shuddered at the memory of Holmes blowing up a giant hole in the living room wall once while conducting an experiment. He knew

flip(ped) (動) 翻動　　grenade(s) (名) 手榴彈　　wholeheartedly (副) 全心全意地
shudder(ed) (動) 顫抖

too well that his old partner could get pretty crazy sometimes.

As though he could read Watson's mind, Holmes gave Watson's shoulder a forceful **slap** and said, "An honourable man must never **go back on** his word. Regrets are too late now. Let's ask the landlady to prepare an early supper so we can leave on time."

slap (名) 拍打　　go back on (片語動) 反口、反悔

The Whereabouts
of the Photo

After supper, the two men hopped into a carriage then got off at a place near Briony Lodge at around six o'clock.

Holmes pulled Watson to a dark street corner and pointed discreetly at a two-storey house not too far away, "That is where Irene Adler lives. The carriage taking her home from her concert should arrive later at around seven o'clock. We shall take action at that time."

"What kind of action?" asked Watson.

"You must carry out your task as planned. No matter what happens, remember that you must remain <u>neutral</u>. Do not do anything beyond what I'm asking you to do."

"I understand. So what sort of task are you asking me to do? Can you tell me now?" Watson was getting **impatient** since his old partner still had not informed him the exact plan.

neutral (形) 中立的、不偏不倚的　　impatient (形) 不耐煩的、焦急的

Holmes pulled what appeared to be a short steel pipe from his pocket and handed it to Watson, "Here, hold onto this."

"This is…" Watson was taken aback. "Is this a bomb?"

"Don't worry. This thing won't kill anybody," said Holmes with a cunning smile. "After Irene Adler's carriage stops in front of Briony Lodge, she will invite me into her home and tell me where she has placed the photo. As soon as I step into her house, the window in the living room on the first floor will open. That's when you should toss this thing through the window." Holmes pointed at the short steel pipe in Watson's hand as he spoke.

Filled with doubts and questions upon hearing Holmes's words, Watson asked, "Why would Irene Adler invite you into her house? Why would she tell you where she is hiding the photograph? And most importantly, what exactly is this pipe that looks like a stick of dynamite?"

"You don't have to worry about that right now.

dynamite (名) 炸藥

Just do as you're told." Holmes then repeated his instructions, "Remember! Don't do anything beyond your assigned task."

"Okay, I got it," agreed Watson *hesitantly*.

"We have an hour to spare. I must run off now, as I still need to make other arrangements. Please return here before 6:50 and follow through with the plan." On that note, Holmes quickly walked off and disappeared at the turn of the street corner.

Since it was still rather early, Watson **bided his time** at a nearby coffee shop with a newspaper and a cup of tea. At 6:50, he returned to the street corner across from Briony Lodge, just as Holmes had instructed. Besides a few idlers smoking and chatting near a lamppost, nothing seemed unusual under the dark, evening sky. However, Holmes was nowhere in sight.

How come Holmes isn't here yet? Just when Watson was beginning to wonder, a four-wheel carriage pulled to a stop in front of Briony Lodge.

Could this be Irene Adler's carriage? thought Watson.

hesitantly (副) 猶豫地　　bide(d) his time (片語) 打發時間、靜待時機

At that moment,
the idlers standing by
the lamppost suddenly
all rushed towards the
carriage. At the same time, a

few street kids also ran out from a dark alley. The men and children all gathered tightly around the carriage, fighting their way to open the door for tips.

In the midst of confusion, someone managed to swing open the carriage door and Irene Adler stepped down from the carriage.

"Move over! I was the one who opened the door!"

shouted one of the idlers as he pushed another man who was also reaching for the carriage door.

"How dare you push me! Don't you know that this is my turf ?" shouted the man who was pushed while swinging his fist at the man who pushed him.

confusion (名) 混亂　turf (名) 地盤、勢力範圍

Overwhelmed by the idlers **brawling** in front of her and the street kids screaming and running around her, the **bewildered** Irene Adler just stood there and did not know what to do. All of a sudden, an old, limping gentleman in a blue suit **intercepted** the crowd. The old gentlemen pushed away the **rowdy** idlers and

shouted at them, "How rude of you! Step aside and make way for the lady right now!" The old gentleman tried to clear a path and **escort** Irene Adler away from the **turmoil**, but he was punched in the face after taking a few steps. "Ouch!" screamed the old gentleman as he fell onto the ground, blood streaming down his face.

"Someone is hurt!" shouted a voice in the crowd. Upon hearing those words, the idlers and the street kids all **scattered** away from the chaos.

A tiny black shadow passed by Watson and greeted in a whisper, "Good evening, Doctor."

brawling (名) 爭吵、打鬥　bewildered (形) 困惑的、不知所措的
intercept(ed) (動) 攔截　rowdy (形) 喧鬧的、粗暴的　escort (動) 護送、陪同
turmoil (名) 混亂、騷動　scatter(ed) (動) 散開

That voice sounded familiar. Could that be Bunny? It was only then that Watson finally realised what was going on. *Is this shenanigan devised by Holmes?* But Watson had no time to think back on the details, because he must stay focus on the developments of the situation in front of him.

At this moment, another gentleman ran towards the old gentleman who fell on the ground and said to Irene Adler, "Ma'am, this benevolent, old gentleman is hurt. I don't think we should leave him out here on the cold street."

"You are right. Please take him inside my home. I will ask someone to dress his wound." A kind and gentle soul like Irene Adler was more than willing to help this old gentleman who got injured from trying to protect her.

shenanigan (名) 鬧劇、惡作劇　benevolent (形) 仁慈的

Two other gentlemen who happened to be passing by came to help carry the old gentleman into Irene Adler's home.

I still don't see Holmes anywhere. Could that old gentleman be…? Just when Watson was beginning to wonder, the lights in the living room came on and a maid opened the window.

"This is my cue," muttered Watson as he pulled out the short steel pipe from his pocket. However, a sense of **hesitation** started to come over him. *That pretty lady seems like a kind person. Do I really have to toss this thing into her home?* But Watson's uncertainty faded away as soon as Holmes's instructions began to ring in his head again, "You don't have to worry. Just do as you're told."

"Okay then. Let's see what you're really up to!"

cue (名) 提示、訊息　　hesitation (名) 猶豫、躊躇

muttered Watson as he took a deep breath then tossed the short steel pipe towards Irene Adler's flat. After several flips in the air, the pipe flew **smack** through the living room window and landed on the floor with a crisp clank. It was only then that Watson understood why Holmes asked him to toss his hat to the coat hanger earlier. Holmes was testing Watson's precision in throwing an object to a specific target!

"Fire! Help!" sounded a loud scream that startled Watson's train of thought. Steadying his eyes for a good look, Watson could see thick clouds of smoke rising inside the living room.

"Fire! Fire!" screamed the passers-by on the street in a panic when they also noticed the thick clouds of smoke.

*Was that an **incendiary bomb** that I just tossed into the house?* worried Watson as he stood on a dark street corner watching

---

smack (副) 正好　crisp (形) 清脆的　clank (名) 噹啷聲　precision (名) 準確度
startle(d) (動) 使受驚、使嚇一跳　steady(ing) (動) 鎮定下來
incendiary bomb (形+名) 燃燒彈

the smoke *gushing* from the window. But Holmes's words began to ring in his head again, "No matter what happens, remember that you must remain neutral."

Ten minutes later, the smoke began to **dissipate**. Seeing no signs of an actual flame, Watson felt relieved, his racing heart finally able to calm down. All of a sudden, a head poked out from behind the wall where Watson was standing and said, "Mission accomplished. Let's go."

Watson turned around for a look. Standing behind him was none other than the old gentleman who was carried into Irene Adler's home a moment ago.

"The grenade tossing skills that you've acquired in the army hasn't gone **rusty** at all. Your timing was impeccable too. Our collaboration was **seamless**," said the old gentleman with a wide grin. Without a doubt, this was Holmes's signature grin.

"So it really was you! Why didn't you tell me about

gush(ing) (動) 湧出　dissipate (動) 消散　accomplish(ed) (動) 達到、完成
rusty (形) 生疏的、荒廢的　impeccable (形) 無可挑剔的　seamless (形) 天衣無縫的

the plan ahead of time? I broke out in a frantic sweat just now," complained Watson.

"Not telling you ahead of time is for your own good."

"What's the logic in that?"

"If I were to tell you ahead of time that the short steel pipe was a smoke bomb, would an honourable man like you be willing to frighten a fair lady with such dirty means? But now, you can say that you were tricked by that despicable Sherlock Holmes, so there's no need to blame yourself for anything."

"That despicable Sherlock Holmes? You sounded as though you're talking about someone else and not yourself," said Watson, rolling his eyes.

Pretending to be oblivious, Holmes scratched his head then looked up at the moon hanging in the sky and said, "Wow! Look how beautiful the moon is tonight."

"Never mind." Watson shook his head and gave up. He knew that arguing with Holmes would lead to nowhere.

"So have you found the photo?" asked Watson instead.

frantic (形) 慌張的　despicable (形) 卑鄙的　oblivious (形) 沒注意到、不知情
scratch(ed) (動) 抓癢、搔癢

"I know where it is hidden, but I didn't take it."

"How did you find out?"

"She told me."

"That's impossible."

"It's true. She didn't tell me with her words but with her actions."

"I don't understand. Can you be more specific?"

"It's very simple. What happened just now was nothing but an act. Those idlers and street kids who gathered around the carriage and those gentlemen who carried me into her home were all temporary actors that I've hired. The main character was the old gentleman, played by **yours truly**. Since we received such a **generous** sum of deposit, I went ahead and produced a **grand spectacle**."

"I figured that much, since I saw Bunny."

Holmes let out a light chuckle and continued, "When I fell down on the ground, I quickly **slapped** some red paint onto my face and pretended that I was wounded. Once I was inside the living room, one of the gentlemen who carried me suggested that fresh air would be good

yours truly (片語) 本人(自己的謙稱)　　generous (形) 豐厚的
grand spectacle (形+名) 壯觀的表演　　slap(ped) (動) 塗抹

for me, so Irene Adler's maid went to open the window. Needless to say, that gentleman's suggestion was *scripted* by me."

"I see."

"Then you tossed the smoke bomb into the living room. Seeing the clouds of smoke, the gentlemen who carried me began to yell, 'Fire!' and ran for the front door. Thinking that it was a real fire, Irene Adler *frantically* ran to a door connecting to the living room and opened a secret compartment on the door. You must understand that people will always try to protect the things which are dearest to them in a crisis situation. Irene Adler might be a clever woman, but she was no exception, so she stepped right into my trap."

script(ed) (動) 編劇　frantically (副) 瘋狂地、拚命地、慌張地
secret compartment (名) 暗格　dearest (形) 最珍貴的、最寶貝的

"Why didn't you take the photo then?" asked Watson.

"Although I'm not an honourable man like you, I still consider myself a gentleman. I can't be a **brute** and grab something right out of a woman's hands. Not to mention that stealing is breaking the law."

"So you are fine with me breaking the law but you don't want to break the law yourself? Isn't that being **hypocritical**?" questioned Watson.

"Tossing a smoke bomb can be considered as a **prank** but robbery is a criminal offence which could result in a jail sentence. They're **categorically** different."

Although the reasoning was utterly *absurd*, Watson knew that there was no point to keep on arguing. Far more interested in the ending of the spectacle instead, Watson asked, "So you didn't steal the photo. What happened next?"

"In the mist of the turmoil, I deliberately kicked the steel pipe to her feet to let her know that it was nothing but a smoke bomb."

"What was her reaction?"

---

brute (名) 可惡的人　　hypocritical (形) 虛偽的　　prank (名) 惡作劇
categorically (副) 絕對地、不能相提並論　　absurd (形) 荒謬的、不合理的　　mist (名) 煙霧

"She closed the secret compartment immediately then turned around to look at me."

"Were you still pretending to be unconscious?"

"No. I pretended that the choking smoke had woken me up. My eyes were closed and I was coughing like mad. Seeing that I had *regained my consciousness and that my wound did not look serious, she let me leave her house by myself."

"Sounds like everything went smoothly as planned." Watson might not have agreed with his old partner's way of approaching this matter, but he could not help but admire Holmes's precise calculations.

"So what should we do next?" asked Watson.

"We shall find that burly king right away, tell him what happened just now and collect the rest of our fees

regain(ed) (動) 恢復

for completing the mission."

"But we don't have the photo yet."

"That's not my responsibility," said Holmes **matter-of-factly**.

"What? You're not going to bring the photo to the king?" asked the surprised Watson.

With a cunning smile, Holmes replied, "I never said I would steal for the king. I've only agreed to investigate the whereabouts of the photo."

matter-of-factly (副) 直截了當地

"Oh…" uttered the **dumbfounded** Watson. Thinking back on Holmes's conversation with the king, Holmes had indeed never said he would steal the photo for the king, not to mention that stealing was not **in tune with** Holmes's principles. Holmes would never steal from someone upon a client's request, not even if it was just a photograph.

"Don't you worry, my dear friend. Once the king knows where exactly the photo is hidden, he can find a way to retrieve it himself," said Holmes. "We shall just stand aside and enjoy the show."

dumbfounded (形) 嚇得目瞪口呆   in tune with (習) 與……相符、與……協調

The Uninvited Guest

Holmes and Watson hailed a carriage to The Langham Hotel where the King of Bohemia was staying. After Holmes had recounted the course of events in detail, the king seemed very pleased, "Well done, Mr. Holmes. You shall be granted one thousand pounds once the photo is retrieved."

Holmes assumed his pretentious tone again, "Actually, one thousand pounds is short of being sufficient, but given the honour of providing service to Your Majesty, I shall gladly accept this amount. Let's head over together to the pretty lady's home tomorrow early in the morning. As soon as I point out exactly where the photo is hidden, she will have no choice but to hand it over."

"That's right. And if she were still unwilling to surrender the photo, we shall take it by force," said the king, rubbing his fists eagerly while a **vicious glimmer**

recount(ed) (動) 描述　　sufficient (形) 足夠　　surrender (動) 交出
vicious glimmer (形+名) 目露兇光

flashed across his eyes.

Watson might not have noticed the king's *menacing* expression that only surfaced for a second, but nothing could escape Holmes and his hawk-eyed vision.

"Your Majesty, we shall retire back to Baker Street now and return here tomorrow morning at eight o'clock," said Holmes as he politely shook hands with the king. Kings normally did not shake hands with common people, but this king made an exception and shook hands heartily with our great detective as a gesture of appreciation and respect.

menacing (形) 陰險的、威嚇的　　hawk-eyed (形) 目光銳利的
gesture of (名+介) 為表示

During their ride back home, Holmes was **uncharacteristically** quiet. He seemed to be deep in thought while staring at his own tightly held palms.

"What is it? Is there a problem?" queried Watson curiously.

"It's the king. When he learnt the whereabouts of the photo just now, his eyes had a vicious look that I find rather disturbing."

"You're worrying too much. Perhaps the king was just too excited."

"Perhaps. But it's okay. I have a way to **verify** my suspicion anyway," said Holmes.

At this moment, their carriage had pulled to a stop in front of their home on Baker Street. After stepping out from the carriage, Holmes looked up and noticed something odd, "Watson, did we not switch

off the lights when we left the flat?"

Watson raised his head to look at the second floor and saw the flat's window **dimly** lit. He shook his head and said, "No, I remember switching off the lights. Maybe the landlady left them on by accident after cleaning the flat."

"We better be careful. Don't make a noise when we go up," whispered Holmes. Taken aback by Holmes's heightened cautiousness, an ominous feeling began to *loom over* Watson.

The two men **tiptoed** their way up the stairs. Once they reached the front door, Holmes pulled out his revolver then signalled Watson with a tacit look – *Let's burst in and surprise the intruder* !

Holmes could sense that someone was in the living room as soon as he opened the front door. Without any hesitation, Holmes immediately raised his revolver and pointed it forward.

"Sherlock Holmes, long time no see," sounded a calm, deep male voice.

---

dimly (副) 暗淡地　　ominous (形) 不祥的　　loom over (動+介) 逼近
tiptoe(d) (動) 靜靜地走、踮起腳尖走　　intruder (名) 不速之客、闖入者

Only then did Holmes and Watson notice a man in a black cape sitting on the sofa in the living room with his face down. "Who are you? Why have you broken into our flat?" asked Holmes cautiously.

cape (名) 斗篷

Watson was stunned speechless when the intruder slowly lifted his head, because the intruder was wearing the same kind of mask as that burly king, as well as an icy grin that chilled to the bone.

"What's wrong, Holmes? Why are you greeting an old friend with a gun in your hand?" mocked the masked intruder.

"Lupin...?" muttered Holmes as he lowered his revolver.

What? This uninvited guest is Lupin, the famous French robber? thought the **astounded** Watson.

"I heard that you've been commissioned a big case and have earned quite a large sum of dirty money. I'm here to take a look for myself, how my **righteous** friend have **stooped to** the level of supporting a **tyrant** and

mock(ed) (動) 嘲諷   astounded (形) 震驚   righteous (形) 正義的
stoop(ed) to (片語動) 淪落到   tyrant (名) 暴君

Oppressing the weak."

Although Holmes understood what those words were implying, he nevertheless cringed his eyebrows and asked, "What are you talking about?"

"Don't be daft with me!" shouted the masked intruder. "You are helping a powerful man to **antagonise** a defenceless woman. Isn't that the same as supporting a tyrant and oppressing the weak?"

"You broke in here to give me a lecture?"

oppress(ing) (動) 欺壓　　antagonise (動) 對付

"I wouldn't dare to give you a lecture, my old friend! But I do have a word of advice. If you want to find out the truth, you should hurry over to Briony Lodge right now. You know, you should be

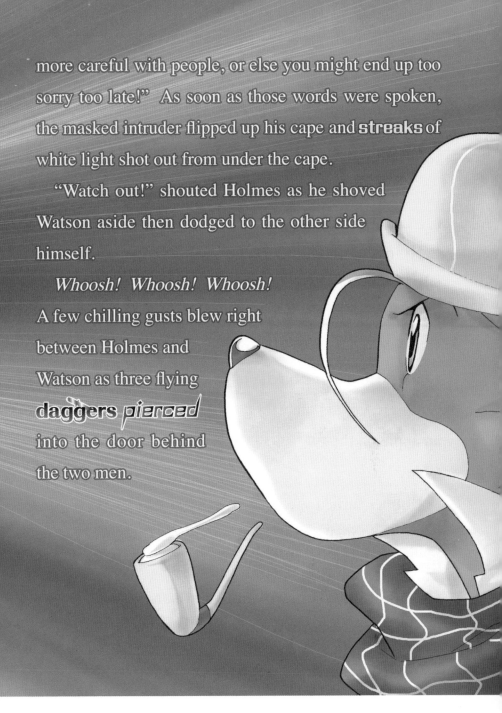

more careful with people, or else you might end up too sorry too late!" As soon as those words were spoken, the masked intruder flipped up his cape and **streaks** of white light shot out from under the cape.

"Watch out!" shouted Holmes as he shoved Watson aside then dodged to the other side himself.

Whoosh! Whoosh! Whoosh!
A few chilling gusts blew right between Holmes and Watson as three flying **daggers** *pierced* into the door behind the two men.

streak(s) (名) 光線　　dagger(s) (名) 匕首、短刀　　pierce(d) (動) 刺

Watson was so frightened that he broke into cold sweat. But when he turned around to look at the masked intruder, all Watson could see were an empty sofa and an open window with its curtains flapping about. The masked intruder had vanished without a trace.

Holmes immediately leapt towards the window to take a look outside, "Looks like Lupin is still as agile as ever."

"What's this?" Watson discovered a half-peeled apple on the table, "Holmes, why is there an apple on the table?"

Holmes turned around and walked towards the table. He picked up the apple and said with a chuckle, "Only Lupin would have the audacity to break into someone's house and leisurely *peel* an apple while waiting."

audacity (名) 肆無忌憚、大膽   peel (動) 剝皮

"No wonder he is one of the most famous thieves in Europe. He just breaks into our home and comes and goes as he pleases with no regard for you at all," said Watson.

"What can I say? When faced with someone like Lupin, all one can do is **throw in the towel**," said Holmes as he recalled his experience with this worthy opponent. "I had a sword fight with him the last time I encountered him in Paris. His skills were so sharp that I was steadily losing my ground. If he hadn't held back, I would've died under his sword. But I must say that I didn't expect his flying daggers to be so brilliant too."

As Holmes jogged down memory lane, the apple on the table caught his attention again. Something seemed odd about this apple, but he could not pinpoint exactly what was odd about it. *

"Earlier, Lupin claimed that you're supporting a tyrant and oppressing the weak, that you're bullying a woman. Was he talking about Irene Adler?" asked

* Can you see what is odd about the apple? Don't worry if you can't figure it out. Keep reading and you will find the answer.

throw in the towel (習) 認輸
jog(ged) down memory lane (習) 回想過去、細味往事

97

Watson, breaking Holmes's train of thought.

Coming back to his senses, Holmes replied, "He was pretty obvious with his words so I'm sure that's what he meant. However, Lupin is a man who loves to mislead his enemies. We shouldn't take his word so easily until we examine this," said Holmes as he pulled a ring from his pocket.

"This ring looks very familiar. Have I seen it somewhere before?"

"Of course you've seen it before. This ring belongs to the king of Bohemia."

"Why is the king's ring in your hand?" asked the **puzzled** Watson.

"You didn't notice me snatching his ring when I shook hands with the king earlier?" said Holmes lightly.

"What? You stole the king's ring?" exclaimed Watson in surprise.

"I had to do it. When we met with the king just now, I suddenly realised that I've made a serious **blunder**."

puzzled (形) 困惑的　　blunder (名) 大錯

98

"What blunder?"

"I hadn't verified the king's identity."

"Do you think he's an imposter?"

"I can't say for sure, which is why I needed to take his ring for **verification**."

"I understand now. If the ring is fake, then the king is also fake."

"Exactly," nodded Holmes as he began to examine the ring under a magnifying glass. The more he looked at the ring, the **gloomier** his expression became.

"Well?" asked Watson anxiously.

Holmes raised his head and replied, "From the light **refractions** of this stone, I'd say this diamond is probably fake."

"Oh no! Are you sure? We can't afford to be mistaken," worried Watson.

"You're right. There's an **infallible** method to test

whether this diamond is real or fake."

"What method?"

"By burning it."

Watson was instantly stunned speechless. *What if the diamond turns out to be real and the fire damages it?*

Ignoring Watson's concern, Holmes removed the diamond from the ring and placed it inside a heat resistant glass test tube. Pressurised oxygen was then pumped into the mouth of the test tube while the bottom of the test tube was set above a fire to burn the diamond through the glass.

Watson held his breath as he stared at the diamond inside the test tube. After around three minutes, the gem cracked open and began to melt.

"Stop!" screamed Watson. "The diamond is melting. We don't have the money to repay the king!"

test tube (名) 試管　pressurised (形) 壓縮　crack(ed) (動) 裂開

Switching off the fire straightaway, Holmes was just as startled, "We've been fooled! Don't forget to bring your revolver. We must rush over to Briony Lodge right now!"

The Ruse within a Ruse

While riding in the carriage, Watson asked, "You said we've been fooled. How exactly have we been fooled?"

"Didn't you see it? That diamond was melting."

"Even iron would melt under such high heat, let alone a small stone," reasoned Watson.

Holmes narrowed his eyes and peered at Watson, "You know, Watson, you might be a good doctor but you can be so ignorant when it comes to science. Diamonds don't melt under high heat. They just transform into a wisp of smoke and vanish into thin air."

"A wisp of smoke? Can you be more specific and less poetic please?"

"Specifically speaking, the chemical make-up of a diamond is mostly carbon. When it goes under extreme high heat, it would vaporise into carbon

let alone (片語) 更不必說　ignorant (形) 無知　wisp (名) 一縷、一陣
carbon (名) 碳　vaporise (動) 蒸發

dioxide. The wisp of smoke that I was talking about is carbon dioxide. I was speaking metaphorically. You're the one who taught me that," explained Holmes.

"If that stone wasn't a real diamond, then what was it?"

"It was glass. Glass melts like that under high heat."

"You should've told me earlier, Holmes! You had me **fretting** about repaying the king for damaging his diamond. I was so **shaken up** that I was *drenched* in cold sweat!" Having said that, Watson felt relieved now that the worry was lifted off his mind.

"That worthless glass ring is enough to prove that the king is an imposter. We don't need to repay him, we need to **get even with him**," declared Holmes.

"But what drove him into **fabricating** a fake royal status? If he weren't a real king, that means there is no royal scandal even if a photograph of him together with Irene Adler really does exist," wondered Watson.

"Which is why I must rush to Briony Lodge immediately," said Holmes. "I'm guessing that this

carbon dioxide (名) 二氧化碳　metaphorically (副) 打個比喻　fret(ting) (動) 苦惱
shake(n) up (片語動) 震驚、煩惱　drench(ed) (動) 濕透
get even with him (片語) 跟他算帳　fabricating (fabricate) (動) 偽造

imposter king is using us to get his hands on something in Irene Adler's possession. That something could be documents or a photo. Also, he seems to know me very well. He knows that I would only go so far as to find out where the photo is hidden but not steal it for him, because that is against my principle."

"I see what you're saying. Now that you've told him where the photo is hidden, he could go and grab it himself, most possibly tonight." Watson finally understood the whole picture.

"Yes," nodded Holmes. "Not to mention that Lupin had come to warn us, urging us to head to Briony Lodge."

"That's what I still don't understand. What does Lupin have to do with the imposter king? Why did Lupin want to ruin the imposter king's plan? Also, Lupin seems to know about Irene Adler's situation like the back of his hand. Has Irene Adler hired Lupin to handle the imposter king for her?" asked Watson.

"Hmmm…" Holmes thought for a moment before

possession (名) 私藏、擁有

replying, "According to my records, Irene Adler used to be a singer at the Royal Opera in France. She has only moved to London about half a year ago. **Coincidentally**, Lupin has also only begun to burgle London these past couple of months. This means that Irene Adler and Lupin have two things in common. They both used to live in France and they both came to London at around the same time."

"Is it possible that Irene Adler and Lupin were **acquainted** in France then both came to London for some special reason?" speculated Watson.

"It's very possible. How else could these two individuals be connected otherwise?" said Holmes.

Wrapping up their discussion as their carriage approached Briony Lodge, Holmes and Watson decided to get off right before the carriage pulled to Serpentine Avenue. Their pocket watches **indicated** that it was already midnight.

"What should we do next?" asked Watson.

"We don't want to **alert** the enemy, so let's keep a

---

coincidentally (副) 剛巧地   acquaint(ed) (動) 認識   speculate(d) (動) 猜測、估計
wrap(ping) up (片語動) 結束   indicate(d) (動) 指示出   alert (動) 使警覺、使警惕

watchful eye at the street corner across Briony Lodge first. We can make our move once we see what that imposter king is really **up to**," whispered Holmes.

On that note, the two men quickly tiptoed over to the street corner across Briony Lodge. The house appeared to be completely dark inside, as though all of its **tenants** were already asleep. About half an hour later, a few shadows slipped out from an alley beside the house. One of the shadows was very tall and big, most likely to be the imposter king.

"There are five men," said Holmes.

"I think they're trying to sneak into

(be) up to (sth) (習) 正在做 (通常指偷偷地、做一些不法之事)
tenant(s) (名) 租戶

Irene Adler's home. Should we stop them?" asked Watson.

"Let's wait and see what happens first. It's better that we know exactly what's going on before we do anything."

"What if they hurt Irene Adler?" worried Watson.

"Don't worry. From what Lupin had told us, Irene Adler should be on high alert. Also, with Lupin as her bodyguard, those five *thugs* won't be able to get close to her at all, let alone hurting a hair on her head."

thug(s) (名) 惡棍、流氓

A moment later, those five men managed to open the front door and sneaked inside the house.

"It's time to make our move." On that note, Holmes carefully slid out of the street corner. But after taking only a few steps, he noticed another five shadows gathering in front of Briony Lodge.

Startled by this unexpected group that appeared out of nowhere, Holmes immediately pulled Watson back to a dark spot at the street corner.

"How come there's another group of men?" asked Watson.

"Very strange indeed." Holmes took a pause before he continued, "Eh? Those two shadows look very familiar."

Watson fixed his gaze for a better look then utter in surprise, "Aren't they Gorilla and Fox?"

"Why are they here?" As baffled as Watson, Holmes stretched his neck to take another peek. The other three shadows turned out to be police officers in uniform.

gaze (名) 視線

Before Holmes and Watson could come up with the best way to proceed now that the situation had changed, a harrowing cry sounded from Briony Lodge followed by a series of knocking and banging noises. Alarmed by the commotion, Gorilla kicked open the front door straightaway.

"Catch him! Don't let him get away!" shouted Gorilla as Fox and the other police officers charged into the house.

"Let's go!" shouted Holmes as he ran towards Briony Lodge. With no time for hesitation, Watson immediately followed suit.

It was pitch-dark inside the house, but shouts and grunts and occasional painful screams were clearly audible.

Concerned that the wrong people could get hurt in the dark, Holmes picked up the gas lamp by the front door that he

harrowing (形) 悲慘的　　commotion (名) 騷動　　charge(d) (動) 衝、進攻
follow(ed) suit (習) 緊隨、跟着做　　pitch-dark (形) 漆黑的
grunt(s) (名) 咬着牙根似的聲音、咕嚕　　audible (形) 聽得到的

109

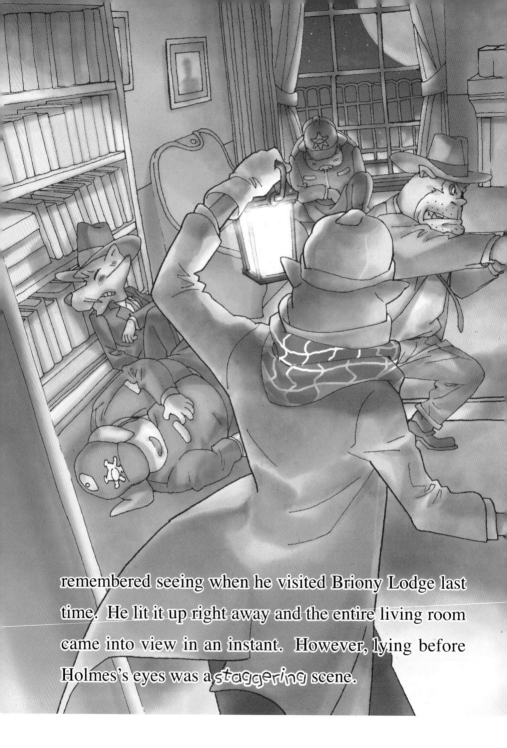

remembered seeing when he visited Briony Lodge last time. He lit it up right away and the entire living room came into view in an instant. However, lying before Holmes's eyes was a staggering scene.

staggering (形) 難以相信的、驚人的

Four thugs and four police officers, including Fox, unfortunately, were lying on the floor moaning in pain, probably from fighting each other in the dark.

Meanwhile, Gorilla, Lupin and the imposter king who was wearing his mask were in the middle of a **triangular standoff** .

"Lupin, give yourself up now! You're under arrest!" shouted Gorilla, though he seemed unsure to whom he should be pointing his gun.

"I am the King of Bohemia, not Lupin. You should point your gun at him!" said the imposter king as he pointed his finger towards Lupin.

Upon hearing those words, Gorilla immediately switched the direction of his gunpoint towards Lupin.

Lupin turned his head towards the imposter king and saw that the imposter king was also wearing a mask.

moan(ing) (動) 呻吟　　triangular standoff (形+名) 三方對峙

The quick-witted Lupin immediately pretended to panic, "I... I... I'm just a petty thief. I'm not Lupin. Look at me. I'm so short and scrawny. How could I be that notorious French robber? Take a look at him. He is so big and tall. Surely he looks more like a world-famous **burglar**."

Taken aback, Gorilla switched the direction of his gunpoint again, this time aiming at the imposter king.

"No, I am the King of Bohemia! He is Lupin! Not me!" roared the imposter king.

"No, no, no! I'm just a nameless petty thief. Lupin is him!" cried Lupin.

Pointing his gun back and forth, Gorilla was **at a complete loss**.

At this moment, the imposter king suddenly noticed that Holmes was also standing in the living room. He pointed at Holmes and said, "I know Sherlock Holmes.

---

scrawny (形) 骨瘦如柴的　notorious (形) 聲名狼藉的、惡名遠播的
burglar (名) 盜賊　at a complete loss (片語) 困惑、不知如何是好

He can **vouch for** my identity. I am the King of Bohemia, not Lupin!"

In the midst of confusion, Gorilla had not even noticed Holmes's presence. He looked over to Holmes and asked, "What are you doing here?"

"Watson and I happened to be passing by this house when we heard fighting noises, so we came inside for a look," said our great detective casually.

Although Gorilla was pretty sure Holmes was lying, he did not bother to challenge Holmes's unlikely excuse since his mind was wholly focused on arresting Lupin at the moment. Instead, Gorilla just asked Holmes, "Do

vouch for (片語動) 保證、作證

you know this big guy? Is he really a king?"

Holmes gave the imposter king a once-over then replied Gorilla with an icy chuckle, "Why would a dignified king visit a commoner's home in the middle of the night? Also, have you ever seen or heard of a king roaming around town wearing a mask on his face?"

"What?" exclaimed the stunned imposter king.

Agreeing with Holmes's logic, Gorilla pointed his gun towards the imposter king and shouted, "Lupin, did you think you could fool me so easily? Be smart and give yourself up now! **Resistance** is futile!"

The imposter king knew that arguing would lead to nowhere, not to mention that it would be far worse for him if his true identity were exposed to Scotland Yard. Pretending to surrender himself, the imposter king

icy chuckle (形+名) 冷笑   resistance (名) 反抗

raised his hands in the air then suddenly lunged forward to tackle Gorilla. However, Gorilla was not a man who could be taken down easily. Gorilla might not be gifted intellectually, but he certainly was very agile

physically. After dodging from the imposter king's tackle, Gorilla jumped high in the air then *whacked* the back of the imposter king's head with the handle of his gun. The imposter king was knocked out instantly and collapsed onto

intellectually (副) 智力上　　whack(ed) (動) 用力敲打、重擊

the floor with a loud **thud**.
Meanwhile, Lupin had slid beside Holmes and whispered into Holmes's ear, "You have a pair of

> Those words sound familiar. Where have I heard them before?

honest eyes.

They shall bring us good luck."

Taken by surprise, Holmes could not help but wonder, *Those words sound familiar. Where have I heard them before?* But when he came back to his senses, Lupin had already slipped out of the window and vanished into the night.

"Where is that petty thief?" asked Gorilla when he suddenly noticed that the shorter masked man was gone.

thud (名) 砰的一聲

Holmes shrugged his shoulders and turned to Watson, "Have you seen him?"

As though he had just woken up from a dream, Watson replied in a stammer, "I… I think…he jumped out of the window." Actually, Watson was not putting on an act. He had hardly steadied himself from all the commotion and confusion happening around him. Too many surprising events had just unfolded before his eyes within a very short period of time.

"The small fish had slipped away faster than the big fish." Although Gorilla's tone sounded grumpy, his face was actually wearing a smug smile. "Good thing we received a tip-off that Lupin was planning to rob this house. We've caught ourselves a big fish this time! We've struck gold!"

Needless to say, that tip-off must have come from Lupin himself, as a plan to shake off his enemy through the hands of someone else. Basically, Lupin had **manipulated** the police force to get rid of the imposter king and his men in one go. Seeing

stammer (名) 結結巴巴地說、口吃着說   put(ting) on an act (習) 裝模作樣
grumpy (形) 怒氣沖沖的   struck (strike) gold (習) 行運了、發達了
manipulate(d) (動) 利用   get rid of (習) 除掉、消滅

through Lupin's master plan, Holmes could not help but admire Lupin's **ingenuity** in devising this clever ruse within a ruse.

After pulling Fox and the other police officers back up on their feet, Gorilla rounded up the imposter king and his four thugs and escorted them back to the police station. Once the other men had all left, Holmes and Watson went to check the secret compartment where Irene Adler had stored the photograph, only to find the compartment emptied out. Needless to say, Irene Adler and her maids had also fled and disappeared without a trace.

ingenuity (名) 聰明才智　ruse (名) 詭計

Lupin and Irene Adler

When the two men returned to their flat on Baker Street, Watson let out a sigh and said, "The imposter king might've been arrested, but we walked out of Briony Lodge empty-handed. We still don't know what exactly is in that photo that the imposter king so *desperately* wanted."

"That is regretful indeed, but at least we earned a large sum of money from this case, so our efforts did not amount to..." Holmes suddenly cut his sentence short as a thought sprang to his mind. He quickly *strode* to the safe and opened it urgently.

"What is it?" asked Watson.

"Oh no! The money is gone!" screamed Holmes.

"What?" exclaimed the surprised Watson.

"Look! There's only a letter left inside," said Holmes as he *ripped* open the letter's envelope. After

---

desperately (副) 不顧一切、拚命地　strode (stride) (動) 大步走　rip(ped) (動) 撕

a quick skim through, Holmes uttered, "Dr. M was behind it all!"

The letter was written as such…

Dear Mr. Holmes,

By the time you read this letter, everything is already over. The gang of thugs that Dr. M had sent over to retrieve the photo should be arrested by the Scotland Yard police officers, and I should be far away from London enjoying my honeymoon with my husband.

You must be completely baffled at how things have turned out. Actually, your little act was pretty *convincing*, to the point where I honestly believed you really were a *manure-reeking* idler when I first met you at the church. But the performance where you staged at my house was a bit too much. You even went so far as to use a smoke bomb as a prop! After you left my house, I followed you and your

convincing (形) 令人信服的、有說服力的　manure-reeking (形) 馬糞臭味

companion to the Langham Hotel and eavesdropped on your conversation with the imposter king. Don't get me wrong. I'm not angry with you. I was just surprised to learn that a great detective like you could make such an elementary mistake and wrongly trusted an imposter.

Although I'm not angry with you, I simply cannot turn a blind eye on your ill-gotten gains. This large sum of money shall provide for the needs of many in dire poverty. I here thank you for them.

You must also be wondering what is so special about that photo that Dr. M's men so desperately tried to get their hands on. I can tell you that it is actually a photo of me together with Dr. M. We took that photo together during the time when Dr. M was passionately pursuing me in Paris years ago. Dr. M had only been photographed a handful of times and that photo was one of them. In order to keep his face a mystery to the world, he must retrieve the photo at all costs. However, I had not expected him to employ your service to harass me. Dr. M is really too clever and should never be underestimated.

---

eavesdrop(ped) (動) 偷聽　　ill-gotten gain(s) (形+名) 來歷不明的獲利、不義之財
passionately (副) 熱情地　　pursuing (pursue) (動) 追求　　handful (名) 單手便可數完的數目
harass (動) 騷擾　　underestimate(d) (動) 低估

Fortunately, Mr. Holmes, you have a pair of honest eyes and I was able to recognise you because of those eyes.

I'm sure you must be dying to take a look at that photo of me together with Dr. M. As curious as you might be, I'm afraid I cannot part with it since the photo is my talisman. However, this other photo is my gift to you, to commemorate our friendship that sprang from discord.

I shall sign off now as you are returning home soon.

"Other photo? The envelope…" Holmes reached for the envelope and discovered a photo inside. It was a photo of a woman from the waist up. Her smile seemed tender and *affectionate* but also cool and cheeky at the same time. The woman in the photo was none other than Irene Adler.

"Ahahaha!" Holmes could not help but laugh out loud after seeing the photo.

talisman (名) 護身符　discord (名) 紛爭　sign off (片語動) 收筆、就此告別
affectionate (形) 含情脈脈

"How come it is Irene Adler?" asked Watson after taking a look at the photo. However, Holmes was laughing so hard that he could not stop and reply Watson.

Watson snatched the letter from Holmes's hands and read it carefully from beginning to end. "The letter is not signed, but from the content of the letter, it looks as though the writer could be Lupin but could also be Irene Adler. How could this be?" asked the baffled Watson.

When Holmes was finally able to contain his laughter, he wiped the tears off his eyes and said, "You still don't understand? She is Irene Adler, who is also the so-called Lupin!"

"What? Lupin is a woman?" Watson was greatly taken aback.

"No, Lupin is a man through and through."

"Then...did Lupin disguise himself as Irene Adler? Irene Adler is actually a man?" wondered the confused Watson.

through and through (片語) 徹底、徹頭徹尾

"No," said Holmes. "It's the exact opposite. The Lupin that we met earlier is fake. Irene Adler dressed up as a man and disguised herself as Lupin."

"How could you be so sure?"

Holmes walked towards the table and picked up the half-peeled apple, "This apple is the proof. When I first saw this apple, I thought something was odd but I couldn't **pinpoint** exactly what it was at that time. But after reading the letter, I suddenly realised that I was fooled by Irene Adler. You see how this apple is peeled from left to right? Only a left-handed person would peel an apple this way. When I

pinpoint (動) 準確指出

had my sword fight with Lupin, I remember he held his sword with his right hand. This apple proves that the Lupin we met earlier wasn't the real Lupin."

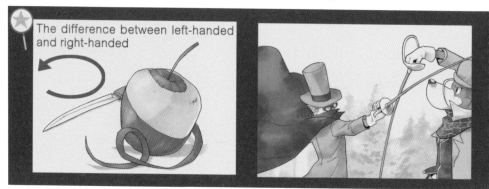

The difference between left-handed and right-handed

"I see what you mean." Watson finally got the whole picture.

"Also, the fake Lupin whispered something in my ear before jumping out of the window at Briony Lodge. 'You have a pair of honest eyes. They shall bring us good luck.' That line sounded familiar, but it was only after I read the letter that I recall Irene Adler saying those same exact words to me when I acted as her wedding witness at the church. That's how I know for certain that Irene Adler is the fake Lupin."

Watson could not help but tease, "You've encountered

the real Lupin in person before, yet you couldn't identify the fake Lupin. Have you gone rusty? It's not like you at all, Holmes."

"Indeed I must reflect on that," said Holmes with a sheepish laugh. "But I think there must be a mystery behind it. Irene Adler is a professional singer so it's not difficult for her to imitate a man's voice, but making her voice sound exactly like Lupin's requires a much higher level of knowledge and skill. Even her moves and agility seemed no different from Lupin's. This is what I have yet to figure out."

"She certainly is a legendary woman," said Watson admiringly.

The next day, news of the arrest of Lupin the infamous French robber

---

sheepish (形) 難為情的　imitate (動) 模仿　legendary (形) 傳奇的

headlined all the newspapers in town. Both Gorilla and Fox flashed their **victorious** smiles in the photo with the dejected imposter king standing in between them. Surprisingly, the imposter king readily claimed himself to be Lupin. Perhaps the imposter king had no choice since he must **conceal** his true identity no matter what. If the Scotland Yard duo were to find out he was an associate of Dr. M's, they would **torture** him to no end just to make him talk. And even if he were not afraid of the police, he probably still would not talk, because he knew too well that betraying Dr. M would only end in miserable death.

victorious (形) 勝利的　conceal (動) 隱瞞　torture (動) 拷問、折磨

Epilogue

Two months later, Holmes was finally able to unravel some of the mystery as he delved deeper into his investigation. It turned out that Lupin had injured himself during one of his robberies in Paris eight months ago. When the French police got word of his injuries, they were so determined to capture Lupin that they mobilised the entire police force into the manhunt. Lupin had no choice but to keep switching his hiding places in order to dodge their pursuit, which only worsened his injuries. When Irene Adler found out about this, she decided to disguise

unravel (動) 解開   delve(d) (動) 探索   mobilise(d) (動) 動員、調動

herself as Lupin and began to burgle around London, hoping to *divert* the French police's focus so Lupin could recover in peace. What Irene Adler had not anticipated was Dr. M commissioning Holmes's assistance to retrieve the photo that he had taken with her. But Irene Adler was a clever woman that could not be pushed around so easily. Ultimately, she was able to outwit Dr. M and got rid of his men in one clean sweep.

Irene Adler was certainly gifted with a brilliant brain and gorgeous looks, but why was she also capable of such agile physical skills? And what was her relationship with Lupin? Perhaps these would forever remain a mystery.

divert (動) 轉移　　anticipate(d) (動) 預料　　commission(ing) (動) 委託
outwit (動) 智勝

Sherlock Holmes Cool Science Experiment
Can Charcoal Turn into Gas?

In this story, you burnt the diamond to see whether it was real or fake. I'd actually like to see what happens when a real diamond burns in a fire.

A real diamond is very expensive. Burning a diamond is no different from burning cash. We can't be that lavishly wasteful.

What can we do then?

Diamonds are made of carbon. Charcoal is also made of carbon. We can use charcoal as a substitute in our experiment instead. The effects will be relatively the same but the cost will be much cheaper.

Brilliant! Let's do that then.

Don't try this experiment at home. Better do it at a school laboratory under teacher supervision. But I can quickly show you how it is done.

---

❶ The following materials are needed for the experiment:

0.2 grams of Charcoal

500 mL Heat Resistant Glass Flask (make sure there is no moisture inside)

Balance Scale

Scale Weights

Alcohol Lamp

Limewater

❷

Insert the charcoal into the flask. Inject oxygen into the flask then close the mouth of the flask with a rubber stopper. Now weigh the flask on the balance scale. (Note: Place a piece of tissue under the flask to prevent it from slipping on the balance scale.)

❸

Light the alcohol lamp and let the bottom of the flask burn in the flame. Once the charcoal is on fire, shake the flask lightly so the charcoal burns evenly.

❹

When the burning finishes, the charcoal will have disappeared with only bits of remnants left at the bottom of the flask. Weigh the flask again using the balance scale and you will see no changes in the flask's weight.

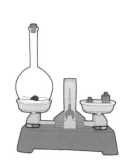

 How come the weight of the flask remains the same even though the charcoal has disappeared?

You mentioned in the story that diamonds would turn into carbon dioxide under high heat. Could this be the same?

 You are right, Watson. When the carbon in the charcoal binds with oxygen, the combination is carbon dioxide. Since carbon dioxide is a gas, it is not visible to the naked eye but its weight remains the same. That's why the weight of the flask is unchanged.

What are those leftover remnants?

They are the impurities within the charcoal. They don't transform into gas.

But how do you prove that inside the flask is carbon dioxide?

 Just pour some transparent limewater into the flask.

 The limewater turned milky when it is poured into the flask. This proves that the flask is full of carbon dioxide.

 Precisely. Limewater is a strong alkaline, which is why the transparent limewater turns milky when it is mixed with carbon dioxide. Isn't it fascinating? A real diamond is not needed to conduct the same kind of experiment. So please don't try to burn your mum's precious diamond rings!

Mask ①

Mask ②

135

THE GREAT DETECTIVE
SHERLOCK HOLMES
— THE MOST FORMIDABLE LADY NEMESIS — ⑫

Author – Sir Arthur Conan Doyle
(This book is adapted from the story of *A Scandal in Bohemia*.)

Adapter – Lai Ho

English Translator – Maria Kan

English Editor – Monica Leong

Illustrator – Yu Yuen Wong

Annotator – Lynn Hall

Cover Design – Chan Yuk Lung, Yip Shing Chi

Content Design – Mak Kwok Lung, Wong Cheuk Wing

Editors – Chan Ping Kwan, Kwok Tin Bo, Lai Wai Han, So Wai Yee

📘 大偵探福爾摩斯

For the latest news on
The Great Detective Sherlock Holmes
or to leave us your thoughts and comments,
please come to our Facebook page at
www.facebook.com/great.holmes

First published in Hong Kong in 2020 by
Rightman Publishing Limited
2A, Cheung Lee Industrial Building, 9 Cheung Lee Street, Chai Wan, Hong Kong

Text : © Lui Hok Cheung
Copyright © 2020 by Rightman Publishing Ltd. All rights reserved.

Printed and bound by
Rainbow Printings Limited
3-4 Floor, 26-28 Tai Yau Street, San Po Kong, Kowloon, Hong Kong

Distributed by
Tung Tak Newspaper & Magazine Agency Co., Ltd.
Ground Floor, Yeung Yiu Chung No.5 Industrial Building, 34 Tai Yip Street, Kwun Tong, Kowloon, Hong Kong
Tel: (852) 3551-3388   Fax: (852) 3551- 3300

This book shall not be lent, or otherwise circulated in any public libraries without publisher's prior consent.

This publication is protected by international conventions and local law. Adaptation, reproduction or transmission of text (in English or other languages) or illustrations, in whole or part, in any form or by any means, electronic, mechanical, photocopying, recording or otherwise, or storage in any retrieval system of any nature without prior written permission of the publishers and author(s) is prohibited.
This publication is sold subject to the condition that it shall not be hired, rented, or otherwise let out by the purchaser, nor may it be resold except in its original form.

ISBN:978-988-8503-91-9
HK$68 / NT$340

If damages or missing pages of the book are found, please contact us by calling (852) 2515-8787.

Online purchasing is easy and convenient.
Free delivery in Hong Kong for one purchase above HK$100.
For details, please visit www.rightman.net.